Row, Row, Row Your Boat

Retold by MEGAN BORGERT-SPANIOL
Illustrated by DAN CRISP

CANTATA LEARNING
MANKATO, MINNESOTA

Published by Cantata Learning
1710 Roe Crest Drive
North Mankato, MN 56003
www.cantatalearning.com

Library of Congress Control Number: 2014938330
978-1-63290-071-5 (hardcover/CD)
978-1-63290-155-2 (paperback/CD)
978-1-63290-389-1 (paperback)

Row, Row, Row Your Boat retold by Megan Borgert-Spaniol
Illustrated by Dan Crisp

Book design by Tim Palin Creative
Music produced by Wes Schuck
Audio recorded, mixed, and mastered at Two Fish Studios, Mankato, MN

Printed in the United States of America.

112016 0355CGS15

More than half of the Earth is covered in water. People use boats to travel across rivers, lakes, and oceans. In this song, two friends learn that life is a dream when they go where the water takes them.

When you hear the chime, turn the page.

Row, row, row your boat
Gently down the **stream**.

Merrily, merrily, merrily, merrily,
Life is but a dream.

Row, row, row your boat
Gently by the **shore**.

Tie the boat up to a rock
So we can go explore.

Row, row, row your boat
Gently down the **creek**.

I will hide among the trees,
And then you'll come and seek.

Row, row, row your boat
Gently through the **bay**.

If we row too far from shore,
We might float away.

Row, row, row your boat
Gently down the river.

If we fall in the water,
We will start to shiver.

Row, row, row your boat
Gently out to sea.

Just the great blue open sky
To keep us company.

Row, row, row your boat
Gently around the **bend**.

When you don't know what's ahead,
It's nice to have a friend.

Row, row, row your boat
Gently on the lake.

Floating on puffy clouds,
Are we dreaming or awake?

GLOSSARY

bay—a body of water that connects to the ocean or sea

bend—a curve in a stream or river

creek—a small stream

shore—the land around a body of water

stream—a flowing body of water that is smaller than a river

Row, Row, Row Your Boat

Online music access and CDs available at **www.cantatalearning.com**

TO LEARN MORE

Jones, Christianne C. *Bella's Boat Surprise*. Minneapolis, Minn.: Stone Arch Books, 2010.

Lindeen, Mary. *All About Boats*. Mankato, Minn.: Capstone Press, 2012.

Magee, Wes. *Row, Row, Row Your Boat; And Ride, Ride, Ride Your Bike*. New York, N.Y.: Crabtree Publishing Company, 2013.

Mayer, Cassie. *Rivers and Streams*. Chicago, Ill.: Heinemann Library, 2008.

Trapani, Iza. *Row, Row, Row Your Boat*. Dallas, Tex.: Whispering Coyote Press, 1999.